Having illustrated numerous children's books, Judy Brown thought it was about time that she wrote some of her own. *Petbots* is her third and latest series of children's novels.

Judy has three children and lives in Surrey with her family and cats.

You can find out all about her at www.judybrown.co.uk.

PETBOTS
SCHOOL SHUTDOWN

JUDY BROWN

Piccadilly

For Sue

First published in Great Britain in 2014
by Piccadilly Press,
A Templar/Bonnier publishing company
Northburgh House, 10 Northburgh St
London, EC1V 0AT
www.piccadillypress.co.uk

A catalogue record for this book is available
from the British Library

ISBN: 978 1 84812 411 0

3 5 7 9 10 8 6 4 2

Printed in the UK by CPI Group (UK) Ltd,
Croydon, CR0 4YY

Chapter 1

Settling in

'I thought everybody had gone home!' whispered Archie. 'Who on earth is that?'

Archie the cat and Sparky the mouse were hiding in the school's stationery cupboard. Archie's radar ears had detected an unexpected person coming up the stairs and they'd dived into the nearest hiding space.

'I hope Flo's okay,' said Sparky. He zipped backwards and forwards nervously behind the door leaving a trail of sparks behind him.

Flo, the third of the Petbot friends, had flown to the hatch in the corridor ceiling that led up to the attic when she'd heard the footsteps. She'd struggled to pull the ladder up behind her. Even with her super-powered beak, it wasn't easy. Just in time, the hatch shut with a *bang*.

Radar ears? A trail of sparks? Super-powered beak? Yes, Archie, Sparky and Flo were not everyday animals. They were Petbots, each with their own special robot skills. They had lived very happily with the Professor who'd made them until he got ill. His house was sold and the Petbots had to find a new home – which they did in the attic of a school.

They'd been exploring their new home one evening, thinking no one was around. The Professor had always told them about the danger of discovery – he'd warned them other people might dismantle them to see how they worked, and would be unlikely to be able to put them back together again. So when they heard someone else in the school, they knew they had to keep hidden.

'What's that noise?' said a gruff voice coming upstairs. 'Some of you kids still up there messing about?'

Archie turned off his torch eyes and hid with Sparky in the far corner of the cupboard, underneath the last row of shelves. They could hear the footsteps getting closer. 'Who *is* he?' whispered Sparky. 'Flo?' asked Archie through their internal communication system. 'Can you see anything?'

Flo opened the hatch
a crack and peeked
through, trying to see
who the gruff voice
belonged to.

'Looks like a caretaker
or something,' she said.

It was indeed. Albert Sparrowhawk, the
school caretaker, walked into the top floor
corridor, carrying an outstretched broom for
self-defence. He had just returned to school after
a nasty bout of flu and was even grumpier than
usual. He noticed the door of the stationery
cupboard was ajar, marched over and swiftly
pulled it open, half expecting to see someone
hiding inside. He carefully looked around the
walk-in cupboard.

Archie and Sparky powered down, desperate not to be discovered.

After a few tense moments, Mr Sparrowhawk gave a sigh. 'Humph. Nobody here,' he said to himself. He'd hoped to catch a naughty pupil up to no good. He slammed the door shut behind him.

With the caretaker still wandering about on the landing, Archie and Sparky were stuck inside!

The caretaker's attention had switched to the messy landing. 'Look at the state of this floor. I dunno, I'm away for a couple of weeks and the place goes to the dogs,' he continued. 'I'll get this swept up, mend that handle on the door of 5A, then it's time for a cup of cocoa, lock the place up for the weekend, and off home. Glad I've got the weekend off.'

When Flo saw the caretaker move in her direction with his broom, she pulled the hatch shut and sat wondering how to rescue Archie and Sparky.

Just then, Archie powered up and spoke to her again. 'We were looking for a more secret route in and out of the attic – I've got an idea how to get out of this cupboard without being spotted! Stay very still by the hatch, and don't move a gear.'

'But why . . . ?' she began to ask. Then she saw a small puff of smoke wafting up through the attic floor. Down in the stationery cupboard, Sparky was using his laser eyes to cut a hole in the ceiling. When he'd got through three sides of a square, Archie used his extendable legs to rise up and stop the section of the ceiling clattering down while Sparky cut through the last side.

'Careful how you aim your laser,' said Archie, slightly concerned. 'I'd rather like to stay in one piece.'

Sparky giggled.

When the hole was complete, Archie said to Flo, 'All done down here. Can you sort out the floorboards up there?'

Using her powerful beak, Flo pulled out the nails in the floorboards that the smoke had risen between, and lifted them away to make a new opening.

'Hi, Flo!' whispered Archie, his green eyes glowing in the darkness below.

Sparky sped up through the hole and parked himself in his favourite spot by the attic window, watching and waiting for the caretaker to leave.

Archie and Flo spent the rest of the evening making a door for the new attic exit and discussing the problem of Albert Sparrowhawk.

'That was scary this evening,' said Flo. 'We were caught off-guard and almost spotted!'

Sparky nodded. 'We thought we'd have the run of the school after home-time, but not any more. And we hoped we could sneak around while teachers and pupils were in class in the day, but the caretaker could be anywhere, at any time!'

'That caretaker is going to be popping up all over the place,' wailed Flo.

'What we need,' said Archie, 'is some sort of early-warning system to make sure we avoid him.'

'Have we got anything we can use in the stuff we brought from the old house?' asked Sparky.

'Not really,' said Archie. 'We've only got the Professor's old computer, a laptop, one camera, his notebooks and some spare odds and ends. We can scrape together a couple

more cameras
but that won't
be enough. I'll have to order some equipment
online, like I used to do for the Professor.'

'There's still some money left in his secret
supplies account – we can use that,' said Flo.

'But how will we get our hands on it when it's delivered?' asked Sparky.

'I'll have to make sure it's delivered this weekend, when nobody's here.' Archie paused. 'And it will have to be signed for . . . but I can think of a way to deal with that,' he said, and smiled mischievously.

Chapter 2

Special Delivery

The next day when Sophie got to school, there was a note attached to her peg in the cloakroom. She looked at the printout and knew immediately who it was from.

'Hey, you two!' she said, calling to Jack and Anya and waving the note. 'Look. It's from *You Know Who*.'

Sophie, Jack and Anya were the only ones who knew about the Petbots living in the attic above them at the school. They had met by accident one day, helped each other out of a sticky situation, and had been friends ever since. They had also promised to help keep the Petbots safely hidden in their new home.

'What does it say?' asked Jack, dumping his coat on the floor and pushing his way through the crowded cloakroom to join her.

She passed him the note. Anya looked over his shoulder and read it too.

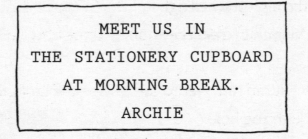

MEET US IN
THE STATIONERY CUPBOARD
AT MORNING BREAK.
ARCHIE

'The stationery cupboard? Why there?' said Jack.

Anya smiled. 'I expect we'll find out.'

So, after the end of morning lessons, Sophie,

Jack and Anya waited until no one was watching, and sneaked into the stationery cupboard. Without permission from a teacher it was a bit risky. There was a creak in the corner of the room and they turned to see Archie's head poking down through the ceiling.

'We've made a secret entrance to the attic!' he said.

The children ran over to the corner and looked up through the hole.

'That makes sense!' said Sophie. 'It's not as obvious as the hatch on the landing. And it's easy for us to meet up in here!' She clapped her hands excitedly.

Flo flew down to say hello and Sparky whizzed along the shelves.

'What's with that caretaker guy?' asked

Archie. 'Where did he come from?'

'Oh, you mean Mr Sparrowhawk,' said Jack. 'He's been off sick for two weeks and now he's back. Miserable old grump, he is.'

'That's a bit mean,' said Anya. 'I don't think he's that bad.'

'Well, he likes you, doesn't he? He's hated me ever since he caught me throwing a stink bomb into the basement,' Jack complained.

'And can you blame him?' Sophie exclaimed. 'It was disgusting.' Sparky zipped over and up the shelves so he was at eye level with Jack. 'Was it *really* smelly?' he asked.

'It was like every pair of the smelliest socks on the planet had been left somewhere really smelly for a hundred years, and then turned into gas,' said Sophie, grimacing at the memory of the pong.

Flo saw her pained expression and covered her beak with a wing to stifle a giggle. 'That was very naughty, Jack!' she said, trying to sound as if she was telling him off but failing completely.

'Well, with Mr Sparrowhawk snooping around, we've decided to set up some surveillance so we know where he is at all times. We don't want to bump into him unexpectedly!' said Archie.

'That would be bad,' agreed Sophie.

'So I've got some equipment on order,' Archie explained. 'It's due for delivery on Saturday morning, but I need a favour.'

'Name it!' said Jack.

'Great!' said Archie, smiling. 'In that case, can you bring me some men's clothes and shoes before then?'

Flo and Sparky looked confused.

'Before Saturday? That only leaves tomorrow,' said Jack. 'I've got Little League after school tonight . . . I'll dash home and get some clothes first and make a detour back here on my way to practice. No problem.'

'Excellent. Oh, and some gloves and a hat would be good,' Archie added.

The others raised their eyebrows, but before they could ask what he wanted them for, the bell rang for morning lessons.

'We have to go,' said Anya.

'I'll come to the gate after school and pass the clothes through,' said Jack. 'See you later.'

'Bye!' said Sophie.

'What on earth do you need clothes for, Archie?' Flo asked.

'You'll see,' said Archie.

Jack delivered the clothes as promised, and early

on Saturday morning, Archie went looking for the caretaker's room. Sparky followed, with Flo right behind him carrying the bag of clothes.

'Right,' said Archie, opening the door. 'Clothes, please, Flo.'

She handed him the bag and watched in amazement as he stood up on his back paws and started to put them on.

'Er, what exactly are you doing?' she asked.

Archie extended his legs so the trousers were the right length, put on the shirt and took Mr Sparrowhawk's work coat from the hook on the back of the door. Finally he put on the shoes and gloves.

'Someone's got to let the van in and sign for the delivery, haven't they?' said Archie.

He drew himself up to full adult height.

Flo and Sparky took one look at him and burst out laughing.

'I guess you're right,' Flo chuckled and flew over to pick up the ratty old hat that Jack had given them. 'There,' she said, dropping it on Archie's head. She paused a moment. 'Wait, there's something missing.'

Flo disappeared out of the door and came back a minute later with the Professor's old scarf. She wound it around his neck. 'That's better,' she said. 'Now your caretaker disguise is good to go!'

Flo went outside and sat on the roof of the school to keep a look out for the delivery van. Sparky zoomed around the playground excitedly, following the white lines for fun, while Archie waited inside with the hand trolley, listening for Flo's signal.

He didn't have to wait for long.

'It's here!' said Flo. 'The van's just coming around the corner.'

Sparky stopped whizzing and waited in the bushes in case Archie needed help.

As the van drew up, Archie got ready to push the trolley outside. He was glad to have it to lean on –  it wasn't easy to walk on two legs, especially with shoes five times too big for his paws.

'Morning, sir,' said the delivery driver as Archie opened the gate. With the hat and scarf covering most of Archie's face, the man didn't notice that he was talking to a robot cat.

Archie searched his audio files for the sound of Mr Sparrowhawk's voice. His built-in digital sampler meant that he could impersonate any voice he'd ever heard. 'Morning!' he replied in the voice of the caretaker.

'Sign here, please,' said the driver, and started loading up the hand trolley.

Archie took the digital notepad with his paws in the gloves, and scribbled as best he could while the delivery man looked in the van for their packages. Unfortunately, his metal paws weren't really designed for writing and he fumbled the digi-pen. It fell to the floor.

'Oops! Butterfingers!' said Archie. But as he bent down to pick it up, the hat fell off!

'Oh no!' said
Flo, watching
from the
rooftop.
'Archie's
disguise!'

Sparky sped
into action. He
zoomed across
the playground
and into the
back of the van.

'What the . . . ?' exclaimed the man, seeing something whizz past out of the corner of his eye.

Sparky dashed behind a pile of boxes and knocked one off the top.

'Hey!' said the man, reaching over to pick it up. 'What's going on?'

Sparky's distraction gave Archie just enough time to hide his true identity and put his hat back on before the delivery man turned round. Archie looked at the digital notepad. His scribble wasn't good, but fortunately it didn't look much different to what anybody else wrote, so the driver didn't bat an eyelid.

And that was that. Archie turned and walked back to the school and the man got in his van and drove away. Which was just as well, really. It

meant that he didn't notice Archie's trousers fall
down halfway across the playground.

The Petbots spent the rest of the weekend hiding the new equipment around the school. Motion sensors, infrared sensors, mini cameras, microphones and pressure pads were all linked wirelessly to the Professor's computer and their laptop, both hidden in the school's attic. They had a spare monitor too, like the one they'd had in the basement of the old house to keep watch twenty-four seven. Archie had also bought an extendable ladder to make it easier to get in and out of the attic. It was hard work, and by Sunday evening they were all in desperate need of a recharge.

'Phew,' said Archie. 'That's a good job well done.'

'I feel much safer now,' said Flo.

'Me too,' said Sparky, settling down for the night.

'Don't get too comfortable,' said Archie. 'It's

Sunday night – backup time!'

Sparky groaned. 'Can't it wait? My wheels are worn out.'

''Fraid not,' said Archie. 'Professor's orders. Complete data and systems backup every week. Come on, it won't take long. You know you always run faster after a backup.'

'Come on, Sparky,' said Flo. 'Archie's right.'

Sparky sighed and wheeled over wearily.

Starting with Sparky, then moving on to Flo and himself, Archie completed their backup.

Then the three of them plugged themselves into the mains to recharge and settled down for a well-earned rest.

Chapter 3

Dodgy Download

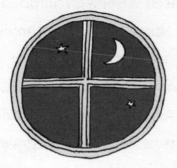

Now they had surveillance they could finally relax. They could keep an eye on everyone, including the caretaker, and they weren't so worried about being caught. They needed to stay in the attic during the day, and sometimes the hours did pass slowly. Archie kept himself busy doing research and sometimes Flo went out of the attic window to stretch her wings. Sparky got the most bored of the three because mostly he liked to zoom around and when Flo went outside he often went with her for a run over the roof of the building. Now they had several cameras set up, though, it made being in the attic much more interesting – they could finally see the daily activities of Sophie, Jack, Anya and their schoolmates. Flo thought it was better than ordinary telly, and she learned lots from the lessons too.

Archie looked at the screen that showed the caretaker's room. It was positioned so that they could see the blackboard that he used to list his jobs for the day.

'What are you up to today, Mr S?' Archie said, zooming in. 'Let's see, *clear up the mess from 4G's science lesson* – oh yes, they were making volcanoes this morning – and hmmm . . . Looks like the loo in the boys' toilet is blocked again.'

'I bet that's Adam. Jack said he filled it with loo paper last time,' said Flo. 'That boy is a bad influence.' She clicked her metal beak sternly.

'Looks like he's got a long day ahead,' said Archie.

'Oh! Crusty cogs!' complained Sparky. 'I was hoping to have a whizz around the hall after school. I haven't had a proper run for ages.'

'You can still do it when he's gone,' said Flo.

'I know, I know . . .' Sparky was not the most patient of Petbots.

The school day went on as usual. Flo learned all about glaciers while Sparky kept himself amused by doing circuits of the attic. It was driving Archie nuts.

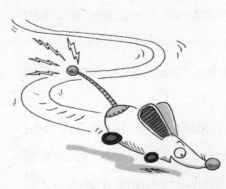

'Please, Sparky, give it a rest,' he said. 'You'll wear a groove in the floor. Come and watch our friends. They're just going into the IT room.'

Sparky zipped over and nestled up to Archie and Flo to watch the show.

Sophie, Jack and Anya were settling down in a row in front of three laptops near the back of the room. The teacher was handing out photocopied sheets of the lesson plan.

'Everybody listen,' she said as she walked between the rows of laptops. 'I want you to work your way through the sheet during the lesson. When you've finished, save your work to the T-drive and sit quietly until I come and see you.'

'This stuff's easy peasy,' said Jack. 'I'm gonna be done in ten minutes tops.'

Sophie smiled. It wasn't that hard but she knew it would take her much longer. Jack had always been good with computers. He actually

knew quite a lot, but unfortunately not quite as much as he thought he did.

Jack was right about finishing quickly, though. After twenty minutes he was done, and it didn't take him long to get bored.

Anya was sitting on the other side of Jack, and out of the corner of her eye she spotted that he was up to something.

'What are you doing, Jack?' she asked.

'Just browsing,' said Jack innocently.

'Careful what you look at,' said Sophie. 'Remember what happened last time. Miss said you'd get a ban if she found you playing online games again.'

'I'm not playing online,' Jack said, 'I'm looking for games to download.'

Watching and listening in the attic, Archie had a bad feeling about what might happen.

'No, Jack!' warned Sophie. 'Putting stuff onto the school laptop from online is even worse. You'll get into massive trouble.'

'Miss Ahmed is too busy with old Porridge For Brains over there. She'll never even notice,' said Jack. 'I can delete it at the end of the lesson.'

'That's not the point,' said Anya. 'There are always really nasty computer viruses going around, and there's one that's really bad at the moment – I saw it on the news.'

'Rubbish,' said Jack. 'I know what I'm doing. Hey, this looks good!'

Sophie and Anya exchanged glances and shrugged their shoulders. They knew Jack wasn't in the mood to listen.

Jack clicked his mouse and leant back in his chair, a smug look on his face as he waited for the game to download.

As it did, his expression slowly changed.

'Oh,' he said.

'What is it?' asked Sophie.

'Oh crud!' said Jack.

'Something's wrong. I . . . . It . . . The laptop's crashed!' Jack was looking rather pale. 'Maybe it's just the browser.' Jack clicked around the screen in a mild panic and pressed some keys. Nothing happened. 'Oh no! It's completely frozen,' he said.

'Oh Jack! When will you ever listen? What are you going to do?' Anya groaned.

'Not so much chatting there at the back,' said Miss Ahmed.

'Sorry, miss,' chorused Sophie and Anya.

'Any luck, Jack?' Sophie whispered.

'Er . . . no,' he gulped.

'Quick, do something! She's coming this way!' said Anya.

Jack held down the power button until the screen went blank.

'Jack?' said the teacher.

Jack jumped.

'Finished already?'

'Yes, miss. Er . . . so I saved and shut down, miss,' he lied.

'Good work, Jack.'

'Erm, may I be excused, Miss? I need to go to the —'

'Yes, Jack, go ahead. I don't need the details. Don't be long, though, the lesson's nearly over and I've got homework to give out.'

'Yes, miss,' said Jack and dashed out of the room.

'I bet I know where he's heading,' Archie said, smiling.

Seconds later the pressure pad in the stationery cupboard was activated and Jack's face appeared on the security monitor in the attic.

'Help,' Jack called up to the Petbots. 'I'm in trouble!' Archie opened the hatch and poked his head through. 'Hi, Jack,' he said. 'I saw what happened.'

'If Miss Ahmed tries to turn on the laptop tomorrow, she'll know it's broken and that I was the one who broke it! I'll be banned for sure.' He had an even worse thought. 'They'll tell Mum and Dad and I'll get banned at home too!'

'I'll look at it later on when the school is empty,' said Archie. 'I've solved all sorts of computer problems with the Professor before. I'm sure I can fix it. Go back to the IT room and try to calm down.'

Jack trudged off feeling stupid, but he was very relieved that Archie was there to help.

When later came, though, the school wasn't as empty as the Petbots had hoped.

'Will he EVER go home?' moaned Sparky.

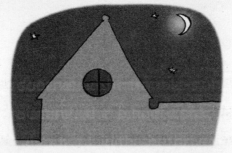

They'd been watching the caretaker go about his chores for ages. 'I'm soooo bored.'

'Yes,' agreed Archie, 'I need to get down there and sort out that laptop for Jack as soon as possible. For all I know, it could be an all-night job.'

'Ooooh! Ooooh! How about I distract him?' said Sparky. 'It will give me something to do.'

'Wait, Sparky!' said Archie.

But Sparky was gone.

The next thing they knew, he'd appeared on the hallway monitor and was heading for the caretaker as he swept the floor – and more specifically, the caretaker's ankles. He did several loops and disappeared off under the broom in a cloud of dust.

'What the . . . ?' Mr Sparrowhawk looked around him. 'Was that what I thought it was?' he said to himself with a scowl.

Sparky reappeared for another pass.

'A MOUSE!' said Mr Sparrowhawk. 'Vermin! I can't have mice in here!' He paused. 'Still, one mouse isn't a problem. I can soon get rid of that.' He carried on with his sweeping and whistled a happy tune to cheer himself up.

'I've an idea too,' said Flo and headed downstairs to join the fun.

She perched up on a beam near the ceiling. She searched her memory banks for a certain film clip and, as Mr Sparrowhawk pushed his broom along the corridor to clean up the dust he had created mending the noticeboard, Flo projected the video through her eyes. It looked as if a huge crowd of house mice had suddenly appeared at the end of the corridor, running over the walls and floor.

'Aaarghh!' yelled Mr Sparrowhawk, and dropped his broom. Sparky whizzed past him down the corridor and Mr Sparrowhawk tried to follow, but when he got to the corner, there was suddenly not a mouse to be seen. He stopped and scratched his head. 'Where did they go?'

He walked backwards to pick up his broom, ready to whack anything that came past. He looked at his watch.

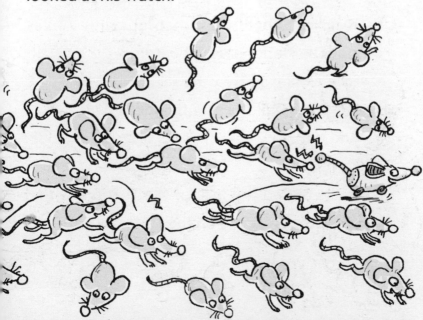

'Hmmm. Seven fifteen – just time to get to the DIY store and buy some mousetraps before it closes.'

So saying, he hurried down to the basement, hung his caretaker's coat on the hook and disappeared out of the building, locking it after him.

Flo and Sparky were pretty pleased with themselves when they met up with Archie outside the stationery cupboard.

'Nice work, you two!' he said.

They almost glowed with pride.

'And now to work,' he said, and set off to fix Jack's mistake.

Archie picked the lock of the IT room with a claw and Flo switched on the light.

'Is it okay if I have my run around downstairs now?' asked Sparky.

'Go for it!' said Archie. 'You've earned it.'

Sparky whizzed downstairs at turbo speed and zipped around in the school hall.

In the IT room, Flo decided to check out the work on the walls of the room. She was especially interested in looking for anything by Jack, Sophie or Anya.

Archie turned on the laptop, pulled out a lead from the end of his tail and plugged himself in to the USB slot.

'Let's see what the trouble is,' he said.

He searched the system for Jack's download. Sure enough, hidden in the game's code was a computer virus. 'You're an evil little virus, aren't you?' said Archie. 'Found your way into all sorts of nooks and crannies.' Archie dug around in the system files, his paws flying over the keys as he typed in computer code to get rid of the virus. Then, suddenly, he stopped dead. His eyes dimmed and started to spin.

Flo glanced over, aware that she could no longer hear the tapping of the keys.

'Archie,' she said, 'are you okay?'

He didn't answer.

'Archie! Have you got cogs stuck in your ears? ARCHIE!' she repeated louder.

He still didn't react.

Flo poked him with a metal feather and he jolted.

'I . . . What . . .? Sorry, Flo,' he said. 'I was a bit wrapped up in what I was doing.'

Sparky returned from his exercise and whizzed over to see how things were going.

'How's the laptop?' he asked.

'Not great,' Archie said. 'This virus is a really

tricky one. It's hard to find and repair all the infected files. Not only that, but it's as if the virus is changing all the time too. With all the computers on the same network, I have a nasty feeling that it will have spread.'

'Oh dear,' said Flo. 'So will all of the school computers be infected too?'

'It's possible,' said Archie. 'I just hope that the main computer in the school office has better protection than these. If that one gets the virus, it could cause all sorts of problems. I've copied all the information I need for now and managed to get this one working at least. But I need to get to the attic and write an antivirus program to search for the virus and erase it for good.'

With that, he shut the laptop down, locked the IT room and they all went back up into the attic.

Halfway up the ladder, Archie sneezed. 'Achooo!'

'Bless you!' said Flo.

'I didn't even know you could sneeze!' laughed Sparky.

'Me neither,' said Archie, a little concerned.

Chapter 4

Bugs in the System

The next day, despite the fact that it was pouring with rain, Jack didn't wait for a lift from his mum and ran to school extra early. He was desperate to find out whether Archie had been able to fix the laptop. He'd had a terrible night dreaming about being attacked by giant viruses and even more giant IT teachers.

The school gate had only just been opened when he arrived. He left his dripping coat in the cloakroom and slipped upstairs to the stationery cupboard.

Flo had tracked his progress from the school entrance, and when his feet pressed on the pressure pad in the stationery cupboard the hatch opened and Archie sent down the ladder.

'How did it go?' Jack asked nervously as he climbed into the attic.

'Well, Jack, do you want the good news or the bad news?' Archie said.

'Definitely the good,' Jack said hopefully.

'I got the laptop working again, but I still need to check it for the virus.'

'Oh,' sighed Jack, looking relieved. 'Thank goodness for that.' He paused. 'Do I want to hear the bad news?'

'Probably not,' said Archie, frowning. 'The virus is a really nasty one. It's likely to spread and it keeps changing. Because the computers are all linked to the same network, the chances are it's infected more than just the one laptop.'

'Which means?' Jack asked.

'It's hard to say exactly. If it's just got onto a few laptops in the IT room, the antivirus program I'm working on will sort it out easily and there shouldn't be anything to worry about.'

'If not, then what?' asked Jack.

'If it's spread to the main office computer, the one that controls all the school systems, it could be much more of a problem.'

Jack could feel his heart sinking. 'All because of me accidentally downloading a virus?'

'I'm afraid so,' Archie confirmed. 'We'll know

more when the system boots up this morning.'

Flo could see how worried Jack was. She flew over and put a friendly wing around him. Sparky zipped over and perched on his shoulder.

Jack sighed. 'Guess we'll just have to wait.' He touched Archie gently on the head. 'Thanks for sorting out the laptop, though. I'll tell the others what's going on. Good luck with the antivirus program.'

Jack went back down the ladder almost as worried as he was when he went up.

Archie continued work on the antivirus program all morning while Flo enjoyed the children's lessons and Sparky watched the rain lash against the attic window.

'How's it going?' Sparky asked Archie after a while.

'Okay,' he said, staring at the screen.

'Archie?' Sparky went on.

'Yes, Sparky.'

'Why are your whiskers twitching?'

'Er, it's because I'm concentrating so hard,' said Archie. 'They always do that.'

'Do they?' asked Flo. 'It looks very funny! I don't think I've ever noticed before.'

But Archie wasn't being truthful – he just didn't want to worry the others. The reason his whiskers were twitching was that he simply couldn't stop them . . . and he had a sneaking suspicion he knew why.

The sound of a high-pitched bell made them all jump.

'It can't be the end of the lesson already,' said Flo. She flew over to the monitor to have a look. Everyone was in the middle of their classes. 'It's definitely not break-time – and why is the bell going on for so long? It usually only lasts about five seconds.'

'I *hate* that noise,' complained Sparky. 'It rattles my circuits.'

Despite the fact that it wasn't the end of the lesson, because the bell continued to ring the classrooms were emptying anyway. But once outside, no one was quite sure what to do.

'Shall we go on to the drama studio, miss?'

asked one of the Year Fours.

'What did you say, Daisy?' asked her teacher. 'I can't hear anything over this blessed bell.'

It was true. Not only did the bell keep ringing, it seemed to be getting louder too. In the downstairs hall, Reception class had been having quiet time.

'My ears hurt!' wailed one of the smallest children and started to cry. The crying set off a

domino effect, and pretty soon the whole of Reception class were sobbing their little hearts out. Combined with the sound of the bell, the noise was horrendous.

'Oi! Stop pushing.' Some of the bigger Year Six boys were now in the corridors too. In fact, most of the classrooms were now empty and everywhere else was crammed with staff and pupils, confused by the incessant ringing.

The Head came out of his office to end the chaos. 'Please, will everyone go back to your classrooms and wait for the end of the lesson!' he shouted.

'What did you say, Headmaster?!' asked the Reception class teacher as she showed her pupils how to put their hands over their ears to block out some of the noise.

'I said . . .' he began again. 'Oh this is useless . . . Mr Sparrowhawk? Mr Sparrowhawk!' The Head marched off in search of the caretaker.

The Petbots were watching events on their monitor.

'What's going on, Archie?' asked Flo.

Archie looked at her and raised a knowing eyebrow. He didn't need to say what he was thinking.

'You mean the virus?' asked Sparkie.

'Looks like we've got a problem,' he said.

The Head found Mr Sparrowhawk in the basement. Luckily for him, he'd found a pair of ear protectors and was feeling quite smug.

'What do we do?' said the Head.

'Do you want the bell to stop?' asked Mr Sparrowhawk, pretending to be surprised.

'Well, what do you think?' said the Head, becoming more irritable by the second.

'I'll have to turn it off at the mains,' said the caretaker, 'but it will shut down the bell for the rest of the day.'

'Do it! Do it now!' shouted the Head. 'Anything to stop this infernal noise!'

Mr Sparrowhawk, with no particular sense of urgency, strolled over to the main fuse box and

 flipped a switch. The ringing stopped. A cheer came from upstairs. 'Ahhhh,' sighed the Head. 'Now we

can get back to normal. But . . .' He paused. 'How will we officially end lessons and call the children in from break-time?'

'There's an old hand bell,' suggested the caretaker. 'I think it's up in the stationery cupboard. Let's take a look.'

But the stationery cupboard was exactly where Sophie, Jack and Anya had slipped into to spend a bit more time with their robot friends. The Petbots had all come down from the attic and Sparky was enjoying being fussed over by Anya and Sophie. Unfortunately, it meant that nobody was watching the surveillance cameras on the attic monitor.

Suddenly the door flew open. Quick as a flash,

Sophie shoved Sparky into her pocket, while Flo and Archie dived into the shadows.

'What are you three doing in here?' asked the

Head, with Mr Sparrowhawk scowling at them from the doorway.

'Er, escaping from the noise, sir,' Anya explained. 'It's quieter in here.'

'Well, Mr Sparrowhawk has stopped the bell, so there's no need to be in here now,' he said. 'Back to class.'

'Yes, sir,' Sophie said. She noticed that the Head was staring at her pocket and realised that Sparky was moving about in there.

She quickly bent down and pretended to do up her shoelace, although in fact Sophie was placing Sparky carefully between two piles of books where he wouldn't be seen. She hoped no one would look closely and see that she didn't even have any laces on her shoes.

A few minutes later, they were back in the

class, where everyone was talking about the bell.

'What do you think it was, miss?' they asked.

'Who knows?' said Mrs Kinsey. 'A computer glitch, maybe?'

Jack winced.

For the rest of the morning, while Archie worked hard at the antivirus program, one of the classroom assistants had been given the job of going round the school, ringing the hand bell at the end of lessons and morning break and lunch time. She actually quite enjoyed it. By the end of lunch, the morning's drama was pretty much forgotten. But the peace was not to last.

Mrs Kinsey's class were in the middle of learning about Ancient Egypt, when . . .

'Pooooo!' said Adam. 'What *is* that awful stink?'

A few of the class turned to look at Robbie, who was famous for the less than pleasant smells that sometimes came out of his bottom.

He shrugged his shoulders. 'Don't look at me,' he said indignantly.

'It's truly disgusting,' said Kate, holding her nose.

Adam's chair was by the window and when he realised that the smell was coming from outside, he stood up to take a look.

'There's a big lorry in the playground. It looks like there's steam coming off it. Hey wait, there's a big argument going on!'

Everyone rushed to the window to see. For the moment, Ancient Egypt wasn't as interesting as what was going on outside.

'It's Mrs Bunting,' said Sophie.

Mrs Bunting, the school cook, was waving her arms around like a maniac.

'Open the window, Adam, so we can hear,' said Kaya.

Adam did.

'PHWOOOOOORRRRR!' chorused the class as a cloud of the revolting smell of fresh, steaming manure filled the classroom.

'I think I'm going to be sick!' cried Sarah, covering her mouth with her hand and running

for the door.

Mrs Bunting, the school cook, was having a heated argument with the driver of the lorry, serving spoon in hand.

'Why on earth would I order a ton of manure?' she shouted.

'I don't know,' the driver shouted back. 'All I know is that I got an

online order for immediate delivery of a ton of prime, fresh farm manure. So that's what you've got.'

'But I'm expecting the food delivery for tomorrow's lunch! I can't cook this!' she shrieked.

'Wouldn't taste a lot different from usual,' said Leo under his breath.

'Not my problem, missus.' The driver shrugged and waved a piece of paper at her, presumably the order he'd received from the school. He walked back to the lorry, ready to press the button that would empty the contents on the playground. 'Where do you want me to put it?'

'I'll show you where I want you to put it!' Mrs Bunting cried. She ran over and chased the lorry driver round the playground, brandishing her spoon.

Flo and Sparky were watching events from the attic window.

'I wonder if there's something we could do to help?' mused Sparky.
'It looks like Mrs Bunting is doing pretty well at the moment,' said Flo. 'What do you think, Archie?'

Archie was up to his metal whiskers in computer code and didn't answer.

'Oh it's okay,' said Flo. 'Help has arrived!'

As the Head emerged to take control of the situation, Mrs Kinsey decided that enough was enough.

'Adam, please close the window. Let's shut out that *awful* smell. Everyone back to your seats.'

'But it's just getting interesting, miss,' said Adam.

'Adam! I'm not asking you twice,' reprimanded Mrs Kinsey.

'Yes, miss.'

The last thing they saw was the Head marching Mrs Bunting and the driver inside the school.

Despite the fact that the classroom now smelled like a farmyard, all of the children were still laughing five minutes later.

All except Jack.

Chapter 5

infection!

'It's just as I feared,' said Archie, when he took a break and Flo and Sparkie told him what had happened. 'The virus has spread to the school's server and infected the main computer. It's causing these mix-ups.'

'It was funny, though!' laughed Sparky.

'I'm glad we can shut off our smell sensors,'

giggled Flo. 'It must really stink down there!'

'Yes,' Archie agreed. 'Still, it seems funny at the moment but it might not be so funny in the long run. It could easily spread to the rest of the schools in the district and . . .'

Archie paused as his eyes flashed and turned a different colour, then he continued, '. . . *puede causar todo tipo de problemas. Sobre todo si es . . .*'

Flo and Sparky were confused.

'Was that . . . ?' asked Sparky.

'I think he's speaking in Spanish!' said Flo.

They looked at each other and burst out laughing.

'*¿Qué te pasa? ¿Por qué te ríes?*' said Archie. His eyes flashed again and went back to their normal green. 'What is it?' he asked.

'You were speaking in Spanish!' Flo giggled.

81

'Oh! Ha ha,' Archie laughed unconvincingly. He felt a shiver in his cogs. This was a very worrying sign.

Sparky suddenly looked concerned. 'Archie!' he said. 'Maybe you've caught the virus too!'

'Me? No, I'm sure I'm fine,' he lied. 'But I will use the antivirus program on myself, just to be on the safe side.'

But Archie knew he *was* infected – and he could feel it getting worse. His whiskers twitched again and he knew it was vital to get the program finished as soon as he could.

'You're sure you're okay?' said Flo.

'Course I am, Flo. Don't worry.' He thought it best not to worry them at this stage. After all, there wasn't really anything they could do.

When school finished, Jack, Sophie and Anya hung around on the upper landing, waiting for everyone to leave before they slipped into the stationery cupboard. Jack was just about to go in when Mr Sparrowhawk stomped up the stairs.

'Oi! What are you lot doing there?' he said. 'Get yourselves off home. I've got work to do.' He was carrying a large cardboard box with *Mousetraps* printed on the side.

'Er . . . Mrs Kinsey asked me to get something out of the stationery cupboard for tomorrow.'

'Takes three of you, does it?' Mr Sparrowhawk said gruffly.

'There's a lot to carry,' said Sophie, smiling sweetly.

'Hmm . . .' He stared at them closely. 'Well, just make sure you're quick,' the caretaker said. 'I want to lock up early. Got a little someone I need to find . . .'

'Yes, Mr Sparrowhawk,' they said together.

They waited until he'd gone past and dashed into the cupboard.

Archie was already waiting for them. He'd left Flo and Sparky watching the monitors in case the caretaker came back.

'What are we going to do?' asked Jack.

'Everything's going haywire. The main computer must be infected!'

'The antivirus program's nearly complete,' Archie reassured him. 'I just need a little longer. The only thing is . . .' He lowered his voice to a whisper so that Flo and Sparky couldn't hear. '. . . I have a problem myself.'

'Not the virus!' Sophie gasped. Jack was horrified. 'Shhh!' said Archie. 'I don't want to worry Flo and Sparky too much but they know something's not right. My circuits are feeling a bit scrambled and my cogs are creaky, but I have to sort out the school computer before we both get any worse.'

'But, Archie, the last thing we want is something happening to you,' said Jack. 'You should fix yourself first. If I get the blame for things happening at school, it's my own stupid fault. You're far more important.'

The others nodded in agreement.

'Well . . . okay,' said Archie, touched by Jack's concern. 'I'll finish the program, then use it on myself.'

Flo stuck her head through the hatch. 'Sparrowhawk's on his way back!' she said.

'We have to go,' said Anya. 'Good luck, Archie.'

Sophie gave him a hug. Jack felt like he wanted to cry.

By the time Archie had finished writing the program, it was very late at night and he badly needed a recharge. Exhausted, he set the program to run on his own system. He had no

idea whether it would do the trick, though. He'd designed it to work on the school computers, not a system built by the Professor.

'It's just a precaution,' said Archie, as he plugged a USB stick into the port on his belly. Flo and Sparky's eyes were full of alarm. 'Don't worry,' he said. 'I'll reboot as good as new in the morning.'

But as they all powered down for the night, nobody saw the warning light flashing on Archie's main access panel.

Chapter 6

Bad to Worse

The next morning, while Flo and Sparky waited anxiously for Archie to reboot, things in the rest of the school didn't start well.

The staff and pupils had gathered for assembly.

'Ahem!' said the Head. 'Good morning, school! I hope today will go a little more smoothly than yesterday, ha ha.'

Jack crossed his fingers. There hadn't been time to check in with the Petbots yet and he was very worried about Archie.

'Today's assembly will be taken by Willow class, who I believe have prepared a wonderful dance display for us.'

Willow class, one of the Year Two classes, was sitting on benches at the front, grinning proudly. They were wearing wings and bird masks they'd made with varying degrees of success. Their teacher was plugging a school laptop into the sound system, and Jack instantly had a feeling that crossing his fingers for luck was not going to do any good.

The teacher clapped her hands and thirty chirpy little six- and seven-year-olds fluttered onto the stage. Their eager faces looked out at the rest of the school as they waited for the music to start. When it did, the front row of children trotted across to one corner, flapping their paper wings, and the second row trotted to the corner diagonally opposite. Then the dance began. The two groups flapped towards each other, weaving their way in and out as they did, in time to the music.

In the attic, Flo was enjoying the show.

'Look, Sparky,' she twittered. 'It's sooooo cute!'

But all of a sudden the music began to speed up. Willow class tried to move more quickly, but despite their best efforts, it was too hard to dance in time.

'Owwww!' said one of the children when

another trod on her foot accidentally.

Faster and faster the music went. The little sparrows were in a real panic now, but they were valiantly trying to keep up with the routine they'd been practising for weeks. Wings got tangled with wings, beaks were bent, feathers flapped wildly.

'Help!' cried one of them.

One little bird fell and several more tripped over him. The teacher ran over to pick the children up.

The rest of the hall was in uproar. It was the funniest thing they'd ever seen.

'Best . . . assembly . . . EVER!' laughed Adam between snorts.

Jack, realising that the disaster was probably down to his virus, became the hero. He leapt to

the stage, unplugging the laptop from the sound system to end the whole sorry affair.

In the attic, Flo and Sparky were also enjoying the unplanned comedy show when they heard a loud click. Archie was awake.

'Archie!' giggled Sparky. 'Come and look at this. It's hilarious.'

'How are you feeling? asked Flo. 'Glitch free?

Not about to start speaking Russian or anything?'

'I'm fine, I think,' said Archie. He blinked a few times, checking if his systems were running properly.

'I can't say the same for the school,' said Flo. 'There's already been an incident this morning.'

'Hmmm. So I see,' Archie said, looking at the monitor.

The school hall was now emptying and the Petbots spotted Jack, Sophie and Anya dashing up the stairs.

'No need to guess where they're heading,' said Flo.

Sophie opened the door of the stationery cupboard and stepped inside.

SNAP!

Something bounced up and whacked her on the shin.

'Ow!' she said. 'What was that?'

'It's a mousetrap,' said Anya. 'This'll be down to Sparky, I bet. Mr Sparrowhawk must think the school is infested.'

The Petbots appeared at the hatch and came down to join them.

'Archie! You're okay!' said Jack. He ran over and gave Archie a hug. 'You finished the antivirus program, then?'

'Yes, but I'll need access to the main computer to get things fixed. But how to get to it without being spotted is the problem. I don't think we can risk waiting until the school is empty tonight.'

Before they could discuss any sort of plan, they were distracted by the sound of shouting. It got louder and louder, then someone was running upstairs.

'Mr Sparrowhawk! Mr Sparrowhawk, where are you?' yelled the voice hysterically.

'That's Mrs Said,' whispered Sophie. 'It sounds

like she's in a right flap.'

'What's all the racket about?' said Mr Sparrowhawk, joining her on the landing near the stationery cupboard.

The children froze, frightened to make a sound.

'The photocopier's gone mad!' Mrs Said exclaimed. She was in total panic mode. 'I filled it with four new packs of paper this morning and when I shut the cover it just started printing and printing. And now the paper drawers are locked and it won't stop!' She paused briefly to catch her breath. 'Random pages of projects from all over the school, worksheets, web pages and for some

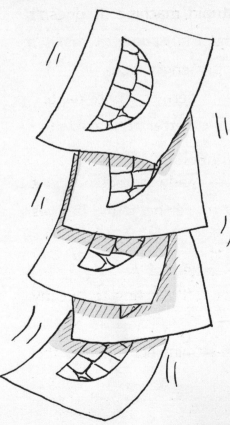

reason masses of pictures of teeth! It's like it's possessed!'

'Calm down, woman,' said Mr Sparrowhawk rudely. 'It's only a stupid machine. It doesn't have a mind of its own.'

The Petbots exchanged angry looks.

'What if she comes in here for more paper?' whispered Sophie. 'You'd better get back in the attic!'

Flo and Sparky quickly made their escape, but when Archie went to move, he found he was stuck! His cogs had seized up completely.

'Go on, Archie,' said Anya.

'I can't move!' he said. 'I'm trying to but my circuits are jammed.'

They all tried to push him but he was too heavy.

The footsteps on the landing moved closer. It sounded like they were right outside the door now.

'Did it occur to you to just pull out the plug?' asked Mr Sparrowhawk.

'Er . . . No, it didn't! Ha ha, silly me! I'll just go and do that,' said Mrs Said and headed off, a little embarrassed.

Archie and the children listened in relief as their footsteps disappeared downstairs.

'Phew!' said Anya. 'That was close!' She put her ear to the door to make sure there was no one outside. As she did there was another *snap*!

'Owwww!' Anya had stepped onto a mousetrap and it was firmly attached to her shoe. 'Owwwwwwww!' She hopped around the cupboard trying to shake it off. Unfortunately – or fortunately, as it turned out – Archie was in direct line of fire and she kicked him square in the belly. The jolt was just enough to get him moving, and enough to dislodge the mousetrap.

'Thanks, Anya!' said Archie, wobbling back up the ladder.

And just in time.

A second later, the door flew open.

'What's going on in here?' shouted Mr Sparrowhawk. 'You three again!'

'We heard what was going on and thought Mrs Said might need some more paper,' said Sophie. She grabbed a pack from the shelf on her way out, while Jack helped Anya hop off to the morning lessons.

Mr Sparrowhawk glanced down at the sprung mousetraps. 'Humph,' he said. 'The little blighters must have got away.'

Chapter 7

Cold and Hungry

In the attic, Flo was fussing over Archie.

'I'm fine, Flo,' he tried to reassure her. 'It's probably all this damp weather. You remember how I rusted up when I got caught in the rain? A few drops of oil and I'll be okay.'

'I don't like it,' said Flo.

Sparky agreed.

'What's more important right now is coming up with a plan,' said Archie, changing the subject.

They settled down in front of the monitors, but Archie was having trouble thinking at all. The virus was coursing through his circuits. It was obvious that the antivirus hadn't worked on him. He knew that time was running out before a full system shutdown.

Down in the classroom, the children of 5B had noticed a sudden drop in temperature. Jack blew into the air. 'It's so cold in here I can see my breath!'

'Miss,' said Amy, 'I'm really cold.'

'Yes, Amy, so am I,' said Mrs Kinsey.

Sophie's chair was near the radiator and she leant over to feel it. 'The heating's not working,' she said. 'The radiator's like an ice cube.'

Jack glanced at Anya. They knew this was most likely another result of the computer virus.

The door opened suddenly and Mr Sparrowhawk poked his head round.

'Heating's packed up,' he said. 'Head says they can put their coats on.'

'Oh dear,' said Mrs Kinsey. 'Are they sending someone to fix it?'

'Won't be here till lunchtime,' said Sparrowhawk, as briefly as ever.

'Go and get your coats, then,' Mrs Kinsey told the class. She didn't need to say it twice.

On his way to the cloakroom, Jack grabbed Sophie's arm.

'Hey! I've got a brilliant idea. I know how we can get Archie to the main computer to launch his antivirus program. Tell Mrs Kinsey I'm looking for my hat, if she asks.'

'Where are you going?' Sophie asked as he dashed off.

'Stationery cupboard!' he replied.

While everyone was busy putting on their coats, Jack headed for the cupboard to make contact with Archie and the others but Mr Sparrowhawk was still lurking outside. Jack waited for him to go but it wasn't long before everyone came back upstairs to the classroom. Mrs Kinsey noticed him hanging around on the landing.

'Come on, Jack,' she said, 'back in the classroom please.'

Jack reluctantly did as he was told.

'What's Mr Sparrowhawk doing out there anyway?' he complained.

'He's mouse-hunting, I think!' said Sophie. 'You'll have to wait until lunch.'

Jack was really frustrated.

The rest of the morning got colder and colder,

and the whole school sat shivering in the classrooms. It was hard to concentrate.

Jack seemed very involved in what he was working on, though. He'd spent the rest of the morning lessons drawing in his notebook, hiding it every time the teacher came past in case she noticed he wasn't exactly following the lesson.

'What are you doing?' Sophie asked Jack.

'It's for Archie,' he whispered mysteriously. 'Part of the plan.'

'I can hardly feel my fingers,' Anya moaned. 'I hope there's soup at lunchtime.'

'Me too,' said Sophie, 'or anything hot. I'm not fussy as long as it's hot.'

It wasn't long before she wished she hadn't said that.

Because of the delivery mix-up the previous

day, the cooks had needed to improvise with lunch, making do with the ingredients they already had.

There *was* soup – but it was cabbage soup. It smelt foul and everybody in 5B prayed that Robbie wouldn't have any. There was cold chicken and salad as well – not exactly warming. The vegetarian option was vegetables with cheese sauce, which sounded tasty until they saw that the vegetables were Brussels sprouts

and – yes, you guessed it – more cabbage. Oh, and to warm them up after that feast, there was cold blancmange or ice cream.

After lunch, while Mr Sparrowhawk was occupied in the canteen, Jack, Sophie and Anya went to the stationery cupboard. Archie and Sparky were waiting for them while Flo stayed in the attic to watch the monitors. They'd been caught out once too often and weren't going to let it happen again.

'I know how to get you into the office!' said Jack triumphantly. 'Here!' He handed Archie the map he'd been drawing in lesson time. 'This map shows the quickest, safest route to the office, and I've marked safe places to stop. If Flo can watch the monitors up in the attic and tell us when it's safe to move, she can guide me and

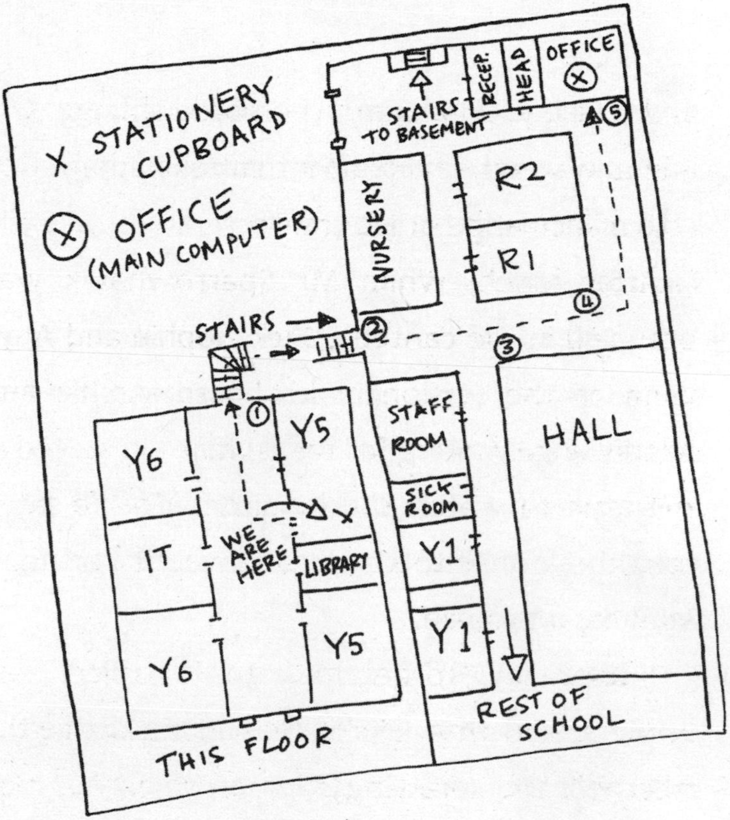

The map illustration shows a school floor plan with the following labels:

X STATIONERY CUPBOARD

⊗ OFFICE (MAIN COMPUTER)

STAIRS TO BASEMENT

RECEP. HEAD OFFICE ⊗

R2

R1

NURSERY

STAIRS →

② - - -

STAIRS →

① Y5

Y6

IT

WE ARE HERE

LIBRARY

Y6

Y5

STAFF ROOM

SICK ROOM

Y1

Y1

③

④ ⑤

HALL

REST OF SCHOOL

THIS FLOOR

Archie there, camera by camera, corridor by corridor, without us being caught.'

'Great idea, Jack!' Flo called down.

'We'll need Sparky too,' he added.

Sparky whizzed around his ankles happily.

'You can help us get the secretary out,' Jack said to Sparky.

'Excellent!' said Archie. He was relieved that someone had come up with a plan as his mind was a blank. 'When shall we do it?'

'First lesson after lunch,' said Jack. 'I'll say I need the loo. After the lunch we just had that won't be a surprise.'

'I'll be ready,' said Archie.

'Mr Sparrowhawk's finished in the hallway,' called Flo. 'The coast is clear!'

'We'd better get to class,' said Sophie. 'Good luck, Archie!'

Back in the classroom, 5B were colder than ever and now they were hungry as well. Even more than usual, they couldn't wait to go home.

Mrs Kinsey switched on the whiteboard while she got things ready for the history lesson. The entire class collapsed into hysterics. She was about to ask what was so funny when she saw that Sophie was pointing at the board. When she turned around, she had to do her utmost not to laugh along with them.

The whiteboard – for some reason unknown to her and most of the rest of the class – was showing a slideshow of the Head's holiday snaps through the years, which he kept on his laptop. There he was with his skinny white legs and knobbly knees, wearing brightly coloured shorts in various locations around the globe. Some of

the photos were quite old and showed a fascinating array of hairstyles.

There was uproar, and the children were beside themselves. Mrs Kinsey tried to load a different page but the whiteboard wouldn't respond. Jack took the opportunity to ask for the loo while she was distracted.

'Yes, yes, Jack,' she said, exasperated. It was proving to be a difficult week.

Outside the classroom, Jack could hear the same raucous laughter coming from all of the classrooms.

'Oh dear,' he chuckled. 'How embarrassing!'

Downstairs the Head was calling for the caretaker in a rather panicked voice.

'Good! That should keep him busy for a bit!' said Jack as he headed for the cupboard and let himself in.

Archie was waiting, ready for action.

'Where's Sparky?' Jack asked.

Sparky zipped across the floor and settled between Archie's feet.

'I'm as ready as I'll ever be!' Archie said. 'You go in front, you know the route. Flo has a copy of

your map next to the monitor. She'll tell me when it's safe to move and I'll give you a sign. Okay?'

'Check!' said Jack, eager to set off.

'Ready, Flo?' asked Archie.

'Ready!' said Flo. 'Okay, the coast is clear. Move to stage one.'

Jack opened the door and they moved quickly to the top of the stairs, with Archie standing right behind Jack in his bulky winter coat, just to be on the safe side.

Flo checked the camera that watched the stairs. They were clear too.

'Proceed to stage two,' said Flo.

Archie tapped Jack on the back, indicating he should move on. Jack and Archie tiptoed down the stairs with Sparky following close behind. They waited under the stairwell.

Flo was already checking the next stage by rotating the camera's view. 'Okay,' she said, 'get ready to move . . . and – No wait! Incoming!' she said.

One of the classroom assistants had come out of a Year Four classroom and was heading their way. Archie pulled at Jack's sleeve and they stepped back into the shadows.

'Phew!' said Flo. 'That was close!'

'Good work, Flo,' said Archie. 'Keep it up!'

Flo did. She followed Jack's map and, using the cameras, navigated them all the way downstairs unseen, right to the door of the main office.

'Okay, Archie,' said Jack, 'you hide in here until the office is empty.' He opened a large wooden chest by the office marked *Lost Property*. Archie jumped inside and Jack covered him with a pile of clothes. 'Sparky, you come with me.' And he picked Sparky up and put him in his pocket.

The school secretary, Miss Pettigrew, was a little jumpy. A nervous person at the best of times, the events of the last two days coupled with the sudden appearance of mousetraps in the staffroom and school office had made her frightened of her own shadow. She didn't like mice. In fact, Miss Pettigrew would have described herself as mouseophobic, if that were a word.

When Jack knocked on the door, she nearly jumped out of her skin.

'Oh! Er, oh come in,' she said, wondering what fresh disaster had occurred.

Jack walked in with a pained expression on his face. 'I don't feel very well, Miss Pettigrew,' he said in a weedy voice.

'I'm not surprised with all this strange business going on. Let me see if you have a fever, dear.' Miss Pettigrew got up and walked towards him, but as she did, Jack let Sparky out of his pocket.

Sparky headed straight for Miss Pettigrew's ankles. It was more than she could take!

'Aaaargh! Moooouuuuse!' she screamed. She ran round and round the room and headed for the door waving her arms like a maniac.

Mr Sparrowhawk was in the basement, but on hearing the screaming, he couldn't get upstairs fast enough. Finally, the mouse had returned! He grabbed his broom and came running. They passed each other in the reception area where Miss Pettigrew was heading for the safety of the

playground.

'It's in the office!' she screeched as he passed
her by.

'Right!' said Mr Sparrowhawk, determined to

catch something at last. He couldn't understand why, despite all the traps, he hadn't even caught one single mouse. 'I see you!' he said, charging into the office. Sparky panicked and whizzed round the room, leaving his usual trail of sparks behind him.

It occurred to Mr Sparrowhawk that this was a

bit of a strange-looking mouse when he came to think about it. Every time they'd had mice before, they were grubby brown things – this one seemed to be silver-coloured and, well, almost shiny. And what was it with those sparks everywhere? He supposed it must be static.

Mr Sparrowhawk swung his broom wildly, missing each time. Sparky headed for the open door and Mr Sparrowhawk ran after him. 'Come back here!' he shouted. 'I'll squish you like a bug!'

Flo was distraught as she watched on the monitor. 'Archie!' she said. 'Sparky's in trouble!'

Archie didn't know what he could do to help without getting caught himself. Then he thought about where he was and got busy.

The caretaker chased Sparky relentlessly around the room, swishing and swiping, each time with more force. Sparky felt cornered and headed for the door but Sparrowhawk got there first and slammed it shut. 'Got you now, you nasty little rodent,' he squealed as Sparky bumped into the door. He grabbed the broom firmly with both hands in preparation

for the final assault, raising it for another wild swipe – and made contact . . . not with Sparky, but with the fire alarm behind him.

Wheeeeooooo wheeeeeoooooo wheeeeeeoooo!

'Oooops!' said Mr Sparrowhawk.

'Oh what now?' said the Head, at the end of his tether, as he came out into the corridor. 'Everybody out of the building!'

Mr Sparrowhawk wondered whether he should explain at this point that the alarm was his fault . . . and decided against it. He'd blame one of the children later – perhaps that strange-looking kid by the main office door. He was clearly a troublemaker to have been sent to the office.

But it was no ordinary pupil standing there. Archie had put together an entire school uniform from what he'd found in the Lost Property box, and had wobbled to the office in order to save Sparky.

As Archie opened the door, Sparky sped over to Jack, who quickly picked him up.

'You two!' said the Head to Jack and Archie. 'Outside immediately.'

'But we —' Jack began.

'I said, OUTSIDE!'

'That's blown it,' said Jack.

Chapter 8

System Shutdown

The teachers immediately realised that this wasn't a scheduled fire drill. However, not wanting to alarm the children, they acted as casually as they thought they could get away with while still getting them all quickly and safely out of the school. The Head was standing in the playground, directing them away from the main building.

'Stay calm, children. Line up with your form teacher for registration.'

Unfortunately for one class, they had been doing PE in the hall when the alarm went off and they were all in their PE kit, shivering.

'We need to get back inside,' said Jack, pulling Anya and Sophie away from the line. Some of the other pupils had begun to stare at Archie, who was doing his best to stay anonymous. Which is not easy when you're a robot cat dressed as a schoolboy.

'What about the fire?' said Anya.

'There isn't one,' Jack explained. 'Sparrowhawk was chasing Sparky and he set it off.'

'We have to register with Mrs Kinsey first or she'll wonder where we are,' said Sophie.

'Good point,' said Anya. So they ran over to Mrs Kinsey to have their names ticked off the list, before circling behind the queue and edging back towards the school with Archie.

There, the Head was busy quizzing Mr Sparrowhawk, and didn't see the children and Archie slip past them and inside the building. 'Did you see a fire, at all?' he asked. 'Or any smoke?'

'Nope,' the caretaker said. He was eager to go back in and catch the mouse. 'Maybe I should go back in, have a look.'

'Absolutely not!' said the Head. 'We must all stay here until the fire service arrives.'

Then, just to add to the general confusion, the heating engineer turned up.

'I hear you have a broken boiler,' he said,

examining his clipboard. He looked up. 'Er, should that bell be ringing like that?'

'It's the fire alarm!' shouted the Head.

'Well, I'm not going in there if there's a fire,' said the engineer.

'Of course not! But I don't think there is even a fire,' said the exasperated Head.

Moments later, two fire engines arrived and the children got excited. With the sudden realisation that this wasn't a fire drill after all, the excitement grew. They gave a big cheer as the fire engines rolled through the school gates, with a police car directly behind.

The chief fire officer leapt urgently out of the cab of the first fire engine and ran towards the Head.

'This is all a mistake,' said the Head, cowering in

the rain, which had just started. 'I'm sure there's no fire. I've no idea why the alarm went off.'

'Well, sir, I'm afraid no one is allowed back in the building until we're completely sure it's safe.'

'Yes, fine,' sighed the Head.

Suddenly there was a loud bang from inside the school and the ringing stopped.

'That's odd!' said the Head.

'Come along, men!' said the fire chief and a group of firefighters went to the door. He went to open it. 'Ooof!' he said. The door didn't budge.

'What the . . . ?' said the Head, pushing past. He pulled and pushed the door. 'It's stuck,' he said, puzzled.

'Lockdown!' said Mr Sparrowhawk.

Archie had told Flo and Sparky through their internal communications system to meet them all in the office, and he ditched his uniform on the way. The room was so hot from the overheating computer that they all had to take off their coats. The main computer had been whirring and clicking away, but after the bang, it had gone completely silent.

'I didn't like the sound of that,' said Jack

'It crashed,' said Archie, 'and it tripped the main power switch too.'

'At least the alarm's stopped,' Sophie said.

Anya had a horrible thought. 'Oh no! Now everyone will come back in!' she said. 'You have to hide!'

Jack looked out of the office to see the fire chief pulling at the front door. 'I don't think so,' he said. 'It looks like the doors are locked.'

'It probably happened when the system crashed. The virus has probably made the electrics malfunction,' said Archie. 'The doors may stay like that until it's running again.'

'Great!' said Anya. 'So no one will find us here!'

Jack winced. 'So if everyone's locked out, that also means . . .'

'We're locked in,' groaned Sophie, finishing his sentence for him.

'Locked in at school,' said Jack. 'Terrific.' He slumped down in a chair. 'This is all my fault.'

'Well,' said Flo, 'technically it's the fault of the idiots who made the virus, but the end result's the same.'

'Flo, Sparky, can you go down to the basement and switch the power back on-on-on-on-on?' Archie twitched. They all looked at him in alarm. 'Where was I?' he said. 'Ah yes . . . When the power's back, we can turn on the computer and run the antivirus program.'

So Flo and Sparky headed for the basement.

It was dark down there with the power off and Flo had to use her infrared vision to find the fuse board. It took both of them to flip the switch, but when the lights in the basement came on, they knew the power would be back in the rest of the school too.

The news upstairs wasn't quite so good. When Archie turned the computer on, the screen was blank.

'Oh dear!' he said. Archie tried to restart it. This time a cursor appeared, and then three words appeared.

Disk boot failure

'What's happening?' asked Jack, distraught.

'The hard drive's been wiped clean. No system, software, school records, homework, reports . . .' said Archie, looking sadly at the others. 'Everything's gone.'

Chapter 9

Back to Backup

Jack buried his head in his hands.

'What have I done?' he said.

Flo and Sparky returned from the basement.

'All good downstairs. The power's back,' Flo said cheerfully.

'Things aren't so good up here,' replied Archie.

'It's a disaster,' cried Jack. 'I'm going to be in

so much trouble. I bet I'll get expelled.' Jack had visions of the police dragging him from the school as his parents looked on, ashamed of their delinquent son.

'There must be something we can do,' said Sophie, putting a hand on Jack's shoulder to comfort him.

Archie racked his memory banks, but they were beginning to fail. He tried really hard to concentrate. He thought about the Professor and how he said you should always try to be logical, especially in a crisis. Suddenly it came to him.

'Wait,' he said. 'A system like this will always have an external backup.'

'Really?' said Jack. 'You're not just saying that to cheer me up?'

'What would be the point of that? I just need to find the link to it-it-it-it-it — My name is RC1. I am a series one robot of —' Archie stamped his foot and shook his head as if to clear it.

Everyone stared at him.

'Archie?' said Flo. 'There's something wrong, isn't there? I know you've been trying to hide it, but you're not yourself.'

'Yes,' he said. 'It's true. I still have the virus. I haven't been able get rid of it. The antivirus I created is for the school computers and it didn't work on me. We have entirely different systems.'

The children gasped. Flo and Sparky looked at each other with expressions of horror.

'Anyway, I can't do anything about it now. I

have to sort out the school system while I'm still able to-to-to-to —' He stamped his foot again.

'Oh Archie!' Sophie ran over to hug him.

He smiled at her and leant his head on her shoulder for a moment. 'There'll be time for that later. I need to find this backup first.'

Archie hoped there *would* be time, but he could feel the virus getting stronger by the minute and infecting more of his files. It was going to be a race against the clock.

'Is there anything we can do to help?' asked Jack, feeling useless.

'Just keep an eye out so we're not interrupted,' replied Archie.

With the operating system not working, Archie had to dig deep inside the computer's basic code for a link to the latest backup. 'This isn't gggggoing to bee eeeeasy,' he said. 'The virus has renamed things and it's hard to fffind wh-what's whattttttt . . .'

Archie's paws slowly pressed the buttons on the keyboard. It was painful and upsetting to watch. Normally his paws were a blur when he was typing on the computer, but his movements were so sluggish that they all wondered if he was going to stop completely.

'Aha!' he said suddenly. 'There they are! The backup files!' He began to type a little faster now he'd found what he was looking for, setting things up so that the computer would reboot from the backup. 'The files are from last week, so they will be virus free. And I'll run the antivirus program to make sure everything's clear. That sh-sh-sh-should do ittttt.'

Before he pressed *enter*, Archie turned and looked at Jack. He concentrated really hard to get his words straight.

'When the computer comes back online, the

doors will open and the staff will be able to come back in. Before that happens, you need to take this USB stick and run the antivirus program on every computer in the school.'

'Every computer?' asked Jack.

'*Every* computer,' repeated Archie. 'It's going to take a while so you'd better start straight away. Flo and Sparky will have a copy of the program too and will be doing the same in the IT room. I'll let you all know when the computer is coming back online.'

Jack grabbed the USB stick and he, Sophie and Anya ran off to start their mission.

As soon as they had left, Archie slumped over the keyboard.

'Archie!' said Flo. 'Are you okay?' She helped him sit up straight.

'Yes, Flo, but we're running out of time. Here's your stick,' he said, handing it to her. 'Now go!'

With that Archie pressed *enter* to start the

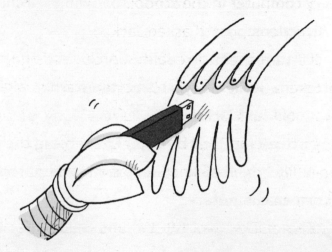

backup, and a stream of data appeared on the screen.

'All I can do now is wait,' said Archie, whiskers twitching wildly.

Sophie, Jack and Anya were moving from classroom to classroom following Archie's instructions.

'I'll turn them on,' said Sophie. 'You run the program, Jack. Anya can shut them down after.'

'Cool,' said Jack.

'Archie's right,' said Anya. 'This is going to take a while. Including Reception class, that's fourteen computers.'

'The quicker we get it done,' said Jack, 'the quicker we can help Archie get better.'

Sophie and Anya had never seen Jack so focused. 'It'll be okay,' said Sophie softly. 'I'm sure it will.'

Jack wasn't so sure. Archie was by far the

cleverest amongst them. If he couldn't rid himself of the virus, how could the others possibly think of something to help get Archie back to normal?

In the IT room, Flo and Sparky were working as

fast as possible. Flo kept checking in with Archie via their internal communications to make sure he was still okay.

'How's it going?' she asked.

'Fine, F-F-F-F-F-F-F-Flo . . . F-f-f-fine.' His voice sounded creaky and weird and she didn't like it.

'How many more, Sparky?' asked Flo. 'I want to get back down and keep an eye on Archie.'

'We're about halfway through,' he said. 'About another ten minutes, I reckon.'

Flo was booting up the last row of laptops when Sophie popped her head round the door.

'We've finished downstairs,' she said. 'Just the classrooms up here to do, then we can give you a hand. How's Archie?'

'Hanging on,' said Flo. 'Just.'

Outside in the playground things were hotting up too. If you didn't include the weather, that is. The Head, the caretaker and the heating engineer had been joined by a technician from the local education authority who had come about the problem from the day before with the school bell. The technician had suggested calling a locksmith to get them back in the building, and now the playground was becoming quite crowded.

'Oh dear, sir,' said the fire chief to the Head. 'Not your week is it? Ha ha ha!'

The Head was not amused. 'I don't understand why we can't get back in,' he said.

'We know the power's back because the lights went on.'

'The lights are on but no one's home,' chuckled the heating engineer.

The Head gave him an icy stare.

'Er, sorry, just my little joke.'

But the Head had long since ceased to be in a jokey mood.

'My guess,' said the technician, 'is it's all got something to do with the main computer. When they go wrong, they cause all sorts of problems.'

'What should we do, then?' asked the Head.

'Break in,' said one of the policemen. He didn't want to wait for a locksmith. He was eager to use the battering ram they had in the police car. It was a new one.

'Is that really necessary?' said the Head. 'What

about the damage? Can't we wait a little longer?' The thought of finding money in the school budget to replace broken doors was not a pleasant one. He rattled the door again. 'Just a few more minutes . . .'

'Better than the place burning down, sir,' said the fire chief.

Flo flapped and Sparky sped from computer to computer, and with the children's help they were finally on the last laptop. There were high fives all round when they realised all of the school computers were now clean and virus free.

It was time for Flo to check in on Archie again.

'Archie, we've finished! You're brilliant! It worked perfectly – there's no sign of the virus on

them now. Archie?' she said. 'Archie, can you hear me?'

There was silence.

Sparky stopped and looked at her.

'Archie, please answer!' said Flo, panic in her voice.

'Xprhfy[8w45345vn.;'#,' said Archie. 'Buhrwt.'

'I beg your pardon?' exclaimed Flo.

What followed was a strange series of beeps and static interference.

The children looked at Flo. Her horrified expression told them that something was seriously wrong.

Chapter 10

Vicious Virus

They sped down to the office as fast as they could. Needless to say, Sparky got there first. Archie looked bad. His eyes were swirling madly, his legs were twitching and streams of sparks were coming off his whiskers.

'Archie!' howled Flo. 'Say something!'

'HBDFUSBKJDFSNJJBSIFA KJF#']38RODSNN!'

'That doesn't make any sense,' Sophie said tearfully. She ran over and knelt beside him. 'What is he trying to say?'

'I don't know!' Flo said. 'Our internal communication isn't working either. Archie, what is it?!'

'MNFDU-OONFJDN!' he mumbled.

'Can you type?' asked Sparky.

'Good idea, Sparky!' said Flo. 'Try to type, Archie!'

Archie managed to press some keys.

D O O R S.

With supreme effort, he pointed at a timer counting down at the corner of the main computer screen. It said **3.30**.

'Three and a half minutes until the doors open?' asked Anya.

Archie pressed another key.

Y.

'Yes!' they all repeated.

'No!' cried Jack. 'We've got to get you out of here before the crowd out there get in. Archie, you have to move!'

Archie got up and tried to walk forwards, stopped dead and then started running backwards. He ran round and round in circles, out of control, going faster and faster and faster until finally he crashed into the wall. Then he didn't move at all.

Sophie was in tears as they rushed over to him.

'We'll have to carry him up to the attic,' said Anya.

'He's too heavy,' said Jack. 'Even between us we'd never make it in time.'

'Wait!' said Flo. 'The trolley! Mr Sparrowhawk's hand trolley! We used it when we took in the delivery – it's just the thing for carrying heavy loads.'

'I know where he keeps it,' said Jack, already running out of the room. He nearly jumped out of his skin when he went past reception.

BANG!

There was a policeman and a fireman with a two-man battering ram attacking the main doors, trying to get in.

'Crikey, that's not good!' Jack ran as fast as he ever had and collected the trolley from the basement office.

'Quick!' Jack said to the others. 'They're trying to force the doors open. We've got even less time than we thought!'

Sparky watched the doors in reception while all three children and Flo manoeuvred Archie onto the trolley. All the while, Archie was giving off sparks of static electricity and the children's hair was sticking out crazily all over the place.

'Ten seconds on the counter,' said Jack. 'Nine . . . eight . . .'

They set off pushing as fast as they could and headed for the bottom of the stairs, still counting out loud.

'Seven . . . six . . . five.'

They were halfway up the first set of stairs.

'Four . . . three . . . two . . .'

They'd reached the top floor landing.

Click.

The doors opened.

Unfortunately, this coincided with the third attempt with the battering ram. This time they'd taken a run at it, and their momentum took them through the unlocked doors and straight into the reception area where they crashed dramatically into a big display of Year Three's class work all

about teeth and dental hygiene.

The group escaping up the stairs had a bird's-eye view of the whole thing and if they hadn't been so worried about Archie, they would have had a good laugh. Instead they headed for the safety of the stationery cupboard, grateful for the chance to catch their breath.

Chapter 11

System Failure

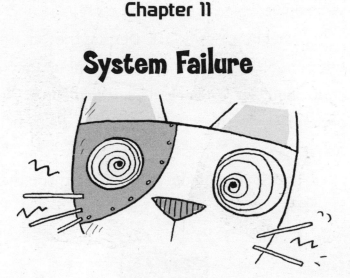

'Heave!' said Flo. 'Heave!'

With a bit of grunting and groaning, the five of them managed to hoist Archie into the attic using the extendable ladder. The sparks were only intermittent now, but his eyes were still swirling alarmingly.

'I hope he doesn't start running around again,'

said Sophie. 'Everyone would hear!'

'So what now?' said Jack. Despite the fact that the school computer and everything that it controlled were back to normal, he was desperately worried. 'What can we do to help Archie?'

Flo and Sparky looked at each other, and then at Archie.

With Archie standing like a statue, his eyes swirling and whiskers twitching, it didn't seem as though he could even hear what they were saying.

'Well, we can't ask Archie, that much is clear,' said Flo.

'But Archie is the computer expert,' said Sparky. 'All we know is what we've learnt from him and the Professor. And the antivirus thing he wrote won't work on him.'

'Is there anything in the stuff the Professor left you that could help?' asked Sophie.

'We've got his video diary about how he built us. We often watch it just to see the Professor again, but there's nothing about viruses on that,' said Flo.

'Hey!' said Jack, after racking his brains for a

good idea. 'What about the Professor's laptop? There might be some sort of repair software on it, something the Professor put on there. Archie might have forgotten about it if his circuits were scrambled by the virus.'

'Good idea, Jack!' said Anya.

Instantly, they gathered eagerly around the laptop as Jack took charge.

'Now where would it be?' said Jack.

He opened a folder labelled *Maintenance.* It contained three icons – a cat, a bird and a mouse. Jack clicked on the cat icon. A window popped up with instructions on how to run the maintenance program.

'Yes!' he said. 'That would help, surely! We just have to plug Archie into the laptop.'

Sparky sped over to get a USB lead. He

plugged it into the laptop and Flo took the other end and plugged it into Archie's belly.

After a few seconds another window opened with a blinking cursor.

Do you want to make a diagnostic scan? Y/N

'Quick!' said Flo. 'Press Y!'

Jack already had.

The cursor blinked.

Working . . .

They waited nervously.

Suddenly the window filled with computer code – and Archie straightened up.

'It *is* working!' said Anya. She squeezed Flo tight.

Archie's eyes stopped spinning and glowed brightly – a little too brightly. The diagnostic kept on running and Archie's eyes glowed brighter and brighter, until the light was blinding. Then all at once there was a *booooof!* Archie's eyes went blank and he shut down completely.

An ominous message appeared on the laptop.

Diagnostic failure.
Databanks empty.
System corrupt.
RC1 is offline.

'No!' cried Flo. 'Archie . . . Archie's gone!'

Sparky sped over in a stream of sparks and hid under her wing.

There was silence.

Chapter 12

The End for Archie?

Jack stared at Archie.

'This can't be happening,' he said. 'What have I done?' He ran over to shake him. 'Archie, wake up. WAKE UP!'

There was no response.

'There's got to be something else we can do,' cried Anya, frantic, but Flo was completely out of ideas.

Sophie was in bits. 'We said – *sniff sniff* – we'd protect you – *sniff* – and now look!' she whimpered.

Anya tried to stay calm. 'We have to think like Archie would,' she said. 'What would he do?'

Everyone looked blank.

'He got the main computer working again,' Anya went on. 'But how?'

Suddenly, Sparky whizzed straight over to the other end of the attic and circled round and round. Flo was racking her memory banks for what to do and didn't even notice.

'Poor Sparky,' said Sophie. 'He doesn't know what to do with himself.'

Sparky couldn't understand why they were ignoring him. He didn't realise that he was squeaking at such a high pitch that none of them

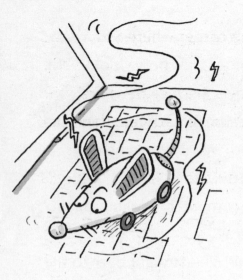

could hear what he was saying. He sped back over to the laptop and danced back and forth over the keyboard.

'Hey, he's typing something,' said Jack.

They all looked at the screen.

BACKUP BACKUP BACKUP BACKUP, Sparky typed over and over again.

'Of course!' said Flo. 'I'm so stupid! Archie backs up all our hard drives every week. Well done, Sparky!'

Sparky jumped up and down with excitement.

Flo flew over to the corner where Sparky had been circling.

'The backups are over here somewhere,' she said. 'Here's the case.' She picked it up, flew back over and laid it down.

'Oh no! It's padlocked,' said Sophie. 'Where's the key?'

'No idea,' said Flo  and sliced through the padlock with her superpowered beak. 'Padlocks can be replaced – Archie can't.'

Inside the case were three hard drives, labelled *RC1*, *Flo* and *Sparky*.

'Now what?' asked Jack.

'I don't know,' said Flo. 'Archie always does it. The Professor showed him what to do. Wait . . .' Flo searched her memory banks and played back the film of the previous Sunday, the last time he'd backed them up.

'All I can see is Archie plugging the backup drives straight into your access panels,' said Anya.

They watched as Archie typed in some sort of code, but couldn't see what it was.

Sophie ran over to the Professor's notebooks, which sat in rows at the side of the attic. She picked one up and started flicking through.

'What about these?' she said. 'Would the instructions be in here?'

'Definitely worth looking!' Flo said. 'You might have something there.'

They all bundled over and started looking

through the Professor's dusty books.

'I can't find anything,' said Jack, becoming disheartened. 'Nothing that gives a clue what to do.'

'Keep looking,' said Flo.

'Got it!' said Sophie.

'Shhhh!' said Anya, reminding them they weren't the only ones in the school.

'Here it is,' Sophie whispered. 'Book thirty-three, right at the beginning. *Petbots – complete system backup and restore.* It says *In the event of a complete system failure the following procedure should be followed* . . . blah blah blah . . . *access panel* . . . It's pretty much like you thought, Flo. Ah! Here's Archie's access code. You have to put that in for the backup to start.

She showed the book to Anya.

'It doesn't make any sense,' she said. 'It's numbers but it's much longer than what Archie typed in.'

Sophie showed Flo.

'I don't know what it means,' said Flo, confused. 'But it's restore code is the key to all our workings. The Professor must have written it in some sort of code to protect us.'

'Let me see,' said Jack. He took the book and examined it closely. 'It's numbers all right . . . Wait, though, it's only ones and zeroes. Hang on! I think I know what it is. It's binary code! The most basic computer language of all!'

'But can you work out how to use it to get the code we need?' asked Sophie.

'Um, I think so, but I'll need some paper to

work it all out,' said Jack, desperate to make Archie better again.

Flo found Jack some paper and Anya handed him a pen from out of her pocket, and he set to work.

Sparky whizzed over and undid the screws of Archie's access panel ready for the code and Flo plugged the hard drive labelled RC1 into the empty port. She pressed the *on* button. Immediately a keypad lit up below the port, ready for the six-digit access code to be typed in.

'Here goes,' said Jack, hoping desperately that he'd got it right. 'I'll read it out.'

Flo nodded and Anya got ready to press the buttons.

'Okay, here we go,' said Jack. '4–8–6–2–1–7.'

One by one Anya punched in the numbers.

There was a quiet whirring sound. Anxiously they all stared at the blinking cursor on the laptop.

'Nothing's happening,' said Sophie, gripping Anya's arm.

'Ow!' said Anya. 'Give it a chance. It's only just switched on.'

Then, suddenly, the magic words appeared on screen.

RC1 *is online*

After ten tense minutes of whirrs and clicks, Archie's eyes slowly opened. They weren't spinning or spiralling and they were glowing their normal green. He blinked a few times, then spoke.

'Hello, guys. Did you miss me?'

Everyone hugged him at once.

'How much do you remember, Archie?' asked Jack.

'Some of it,' he said, 'but there are gaps.'

'I'm so sorry,' said Jack. 'I thought we'd lost you for good.'

'It's okay, Jack,' said Archie, touching his arm gently with his metal paw. 'I'm okay now. No harm done.'

'Eek!' said Sophie. 'Look at the time! We'd better go before our parents send out a search party.'

Flo checked the monitors. 'It's all clear,' she said. 'The teachers have gone home and Mr Sparrowhawk is down in the basement resetting all the mousetraps.' They laughed and had one more group hug before the children went back down the ladder to the stationery cupboard.

'We'll take the trolley and leave it in reception,' said Jack. 'We don't want Mr Sparrowhawk to find it in here. He might start snooping around too much. And thanks again, Archie. I'm sorry I caused so much trouble. What on earth would we do without you?'

The children turned and waved. 'Bye, Petbots!'

'*Adiós amigos*,' said Archie and twitched his whiskers.

They all stared at him in horror.

'Archie!' exclaimed Flo.

'Only joking,' said Archie, and grinned.

Don't miss these other Petbots adventures!

The Great Escape

ISBN: 978 1 84812 348 5

Meet Archie the cat, Sparky the mouse and
Flo the bird – three pets built by a brainy
professor to be the perfect robo-friends!
But without him, their quiet life is turned upside
down. The mechanical marvels are forced to
leave their house and use all of
their special robot powers to
survive the dangers of the
outside world. . .

Coming soon. . .

The Pet Factor

ISBN: 978 1 84812 431 8

The Petbots are mad about
The Pet Factor TV show – pets wow
judges with their clever talents.

The next round of auditions are being
held nearby, and the Petbots are smuggled
in by Sophie, Jack and Anya to get
close to real pets and watch the fun!

But some of the pets are going missing,
and when Sophie's cat is threatened, they
realise someone is petnapping potential
winners. Archie offers to take his place
but will he be able to act like a real cat long
enough to track down the culprits?

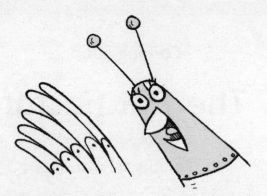

piccadillypress.co.uk/children

Go online to discover:

☆ more authors you'll love

☆ competitions

☆ sneak peeks inside books

☆ fun activities and downloads